The Case of the Yodeling Turtles

SECRET AGENT DINGLEDORF

... and his trusty dog, SPLAT

The Case of the Yodeling Turtles

BILL MYERS

Illustrations
Meredith Johnson

Tommy NELSON

www.tommynelson.com

A Division of Thomas Nelson, Inc.
www.ThomasNelson.com

Published in Nashville, Tennessee, by Tommy Nelson®, a Division of
Thomas Nelson, Inc.

Tommy Nelson® books may be purchased in bulk for educational,
business, fund-raising, or sales promotional use. For information,
please email SpecialMarkets@ThomasNelson.com.

Scripture quotations marked (NIV) are from the *Holy Bible, New
International Version®,* copyright © 1973, 1978, 1984 by International
Bible Society. Used by permission of Zondervan Publishing House. All
rights reserved.

Library of Congress Cataloging-in-Publication Data

Myers, Bill, 1953–
    The case of the yodeling turtles / Bill Myers ; illustrations [by]
Meredith Johnson.
        p. cm. —(Secret Agent Dingledorf—and his trusty dog, Splat)
    Summary: When ten-year-old secret agent Dingledorf is called
upon to find out why animals all over town have suddenly started to
sing, he is reminded of the importance of being responsible.
    ISBN: 1-4003-0179-3 (pbk.)
    [1. Spies—Fiction. 2. Animals—Fiction. 3. Responsibility—Fiction.
4. Humorous stories.] I. Johnson, Meredith, ill. II. Title.
PZ7.M98234Cau 2005
[Fic]—dc22   2004012951

Printed in the United States of America

05 06 07 08 RRD 5 4 3 2 1

For Gloria Walker:
Whose love for children knew no bounds.

"Each one should carry his own load."

—Galatians 6:5 (NIV)

Contents

CHAPTER 1

The Case Begins . . .

Tuesday morning at my place was crazy. (Come to think of it, so is *every* morning.)

Why? Not only do I have three human beings living in my house (Mom, Dad, and myself), but I also have three sisters.

That's right, *THREE*. But it gets even worse.

I have three sisters and . . .

ONE bathroom!

"Come on, Bernie!" Sister 1 (The Prom Queen) yelled at me while on the door. "You've been in there all day!"

"I've been in here six seconds," I complained.

"That's what I said!"

"Let her in!" shouted Sister 2 (The Gossip Queen) as she passed by. "She's only spent two hours on makeup, and you know she needs four!"

"More like forty!" yelled Sister 3 (The Fashion Queen) from across the hall.

After that came the daily clothes fight:

"Hey, you're wearing my dress!"

"Hey, you're wearing my blouse!"

"Hey, you're wearing my skirt!"

(I'm not part of those fights.)

And last, but not least, there was the mad dash downstairs and through the kitchen. The idea was to get past Mom. She'd been up since midnight making the perfect breakfast.

"Gotta go!" Prom Queen shouted as she **ZOOMED** past. "Big test to study for with Sean and Sam and Stan and—"

"Gotta fly!" Gossip Queen shouted as she SWISHED past. "Lots of juicy tales to share about everyone."

Finally, there was Fashion Queen. "No breakfast today, Mom. I need to lose two pounds."

"But sweetheart, you have to eat something."

"I'll grab a candy bar at school."

"What about your fruits and vegetables?"

"I'll put grape jelly on it," she said as she **WHOOSHED** past.

That left me and Dad.

"Well," Dad said then smiled. "It looks

like I'll have to eat the girls' breakfasts . . .
again."

"But honey," Mom warned, "the doctor
said you should watch what you eat."

"Oh, I will," Dad said, digging in. "I'll
keep my eye on every bite."

I joined Dad at the table. I stayed one
second longer than my normal three seconds. Nothing special, just the usual . . .

Two eggs,
Six strips of bacon,
Four pieces of toast, and
Orange juice.

But instead of one glass of milk, I had two
(which explains the extra second).

I got up from the table and grabbed
my books.

I got the required kiss from Mom. (And

gave the required complaint, "Ah, Mom.")
Then I raced for the door.

As usual, she shouted, "Don't forget to feed Splat!"

And, as usual, I pretended not to hear.

I've got nothing against feeding Splat. (Though my pudgy pal could probably do without food for a couple of days . . . or years.) But as a secret agent, my life is *way* too busy for that chore.

I've tried explaining this. But my folks always lecture me about the big "**R**" word.

You know the word I'm talking about . . .

RESPONSIBILITY.

It's the one that makes every parent frown and go into long speeches . . . and every kid squirm and look for a way to escape.

Luckily, I was gone before I had the chance to hear.

Unluckily, I wished I would have stuck around to listen.

School was almost as crazy as home. Almost . . .

"Hey, Bernie!" I.Q. called to me as I stepped into our classroom. "You should (*sniff-sniff*) observe this."

I.Q. has the smarts of a supercomputer—which explains his fancy language. He also has every allergy known to man (and a couple that aren't)—which explains his *sniff-sniffs*.

"What's up?" I asked.

He motioned me to join him at the back of the room. That's where our teacher

Mrs. Hooplesnort keeps all the animals for science.

I walked toward their cages and heard someone singing.

"I'm a chillin' in my coolness,
I'm what's happenin'
From my long, forked tongue
To my shiny skin."

"I didn't know you liked rap music," I said to I.Q.

I.Q. said nothing. He just sniffed.

I came closer and heard a group of backup singers *"Ooooing"* and *"Ahhhing"* with the music.

"Is that a new CD?" I asked.

I.Q. answered with even more nose sniffing.

The singing continued:

"I make chicks scream,
And I munch on rats.
But me and my homeys,
Mostly loves to raps."

I.Q. stepped aside. Behind him was an aquarium. Inside it was our class's pet snake. We called her Sally.

But Sally wasn't slithering around.

She wasn't even sunning herself on a rock.

Instead, she was singing her little heart out.

Wait a minute. Do snakes even have hearts? (Got me. I was more worried about the singing!)

"What's going on?!" I yelled.

But that wasn't my only surprise. Remember those backup singers *"Ooooing"* and *"Ahhhing"*?

I.Q. motioned to another cage that held our pet mice.

But they weren't doing their cute little mice things. They weren't twitching their cute little noses. They weren't running inside their cute little mouse wheel.

Instead, all three of them stood on their hind legs and sang backup to Sally's song.

I looked at I.Q. "Uh-oh," I said.

I.Q. looked at me and sniffed.

CHAPTER 2

From Bad to Worse

After dinner Splat and I joined I.Q. over at Priscilla's house. She's another good friend, even though she is a girl.

But never say she's a girl to her face (unless you want to get beat up).

And never say her name out loud (unless you **REALLY** want to get beat up).

Anyway, Priscilla had just finished changing the oil in her dad's car. We followed her up to her room. It was covered in the usual wall-to-wall posters—hockey players, football players, World Wide Wrestling champs.

"I don't get it." She sighed. "What would make Sally and all those mice sing?"

I looked at I.Q. and asked, "You're not running secret experiments on them, are you?"

Priscilla's eyes brightened. "That's right," she said. "Mrs. Hooplesnort asked you to take care of them."

He pushed up his glasses and shook his head. "I fear I have been (*sniff-sniff*) delinquent in performing those responsibilities."

"Can we have that in English, please?" I asked.

He answered, "I kept forgetting to feed the animals, so Mrs. Hooplesnort hired a company to do it."

"Oh, yeah," Priscilla said. "That's what my folks did with my pets."

"What are you talking about?" I asked.

Priscilla explained. "Since I wouldn't take responsibility for feeding our pets, my mom hired some company to do it."

"No way," I said.

"Yes, way," Priscilla said. "Your mom just did it, too. Lots of families are doing it."

The idea surprised me. Almost as much as my underwear when it started to

beep-beep-beep-beep.

"Uh, Bernie," I.Q. said. "Your underwear is ringing again."

"Yeah." I sighed. "It's Big Guy from the Agency. He probably wants me to save the world again."

"They still think you're a secret agent?" Priscilla asked.

I nodded. "I keep telling them they're wrong, but they won't listen."

beep-beep-beep-beep

"Perhaps they'd listen if you would quit solving their cases and stop saving the (*sniff-sniff*) world."

"I don't do it on purpose," I said. "It just happens."

I.Q. was about to say something when suddenly we heard,

"yodel, yodel, yodel."

I turned to Priscilla. "What did you say?"

Priscilla frowned. "That wasn't me."

"It sure wasn't me," I said as my phone kept

beep-beep-beep-beep-ing.

Suddenly, there was another noise.

STRUM STRUM STRUM

"What's that?" I.Q. asked.

"Someone's playing my guitar," Priscilla guessed.

I wrinkled my nose. "It sounds awful."

Priscilla looked at me.

I looked at I.Q.

I.Q. looked at Priscilla.

Then all three of us turned and looked over at Priscilla's turtle bowl.

It was on the window sill with three little turtles in it.

Well, it *used* to have three little turtles in it.

Now all three turtles stood on the edge of the bowl. They wore cute little Swiss outfits. And in case you hadn't guessed, they were the ones . . .

"yodel, yodel, yodel"-ing.

And what about the guitar playing?
Splat the Wonder Dog sat on a stool beside the turtles. He wore a cowboy hat. And in his lap was, you guessed it again, a guitar that he was

STRUM STRUM STRUM-ing.

Yes sir, between the

beep-beep-beep-ing

"yodel, yodel, yodel"-ing

and

STRUM STRUM STRUM-ing

it had turned into quite a concert.

But it was a concert nobody had asked for.

Worse than that, it was a concert nobody knew how to

beep-beep-beep-beep

"yodel, yodel, yodel"

STRUM STRUM STRUM

stop.

CHAPTER 3

Big Guy Keeps Asking

Actually, it was pretty easy to get Splat to forget the guitar.

All we had to do was order a super-deluxe pizza.

"Look, Splat," I said as I set it on the floor. "It's your favorite. Superdeluxe, with everything on it . . . and *extra* green peppers!"

That's all it took. Wonder Dog leaped off the stool. He waddled to the food as fast as his short, pudgy legs could carry him.

And in seconds everything was gone:

The pizza.

(*munch, munch, munch*)

The box.

(*crunch, crunch, crunch*)

Even the receipt.

(*wrinkle, wrinkle—GULP!*)

Everything was finished. Except for the

BURP-ing.

(Green peppers do that to people . . . and pooches.)

He was still chewing (and BURP-ing) when I finally took him home. I said good-bye to my friends, picked him up, and carried him to my place.

As I walked, my underwear started

beep-beep-beep-beep-ing

again. But I didn't answer it. I had enough problems of my own.

Later, I was in the bathroom getting ready for bed. I turned to Splat and asked, "Are you feeling any better?"

"BURP!" he burped.

I understood perfectly. (So would you if you had extra green peppers on your pizza.)

One of the problems of being a secret agent is all the cool gizmos they keep inventing. I had barely opened the lid to the toilet before a reflection of Big Guy appeared in the water.

"Secret Agent Dingledorf!" he called.

I quickly shut the lid.

I went to the medicine cabinet. I opened it and grabbed my toothbrush and tooth-paste.

Suddenly, the dental floss on the shelf started shooting out of its box. It fell to the

counter and quickly spelled the words:

ANSWER YOUR UNDERWEAR!

I slammed shut the medicine cabinet.

I shook my head. "No," I muttered, "not this time."

I uncapped the toothpaste and squeezed it onto my toothbrush.

BuuuZzzzzBuuuuZzzzzBuuuuZzz

But even after I stopped squeezing, it kept coming and coming! Soon the entire tube had emptied itself onto my toothbrush.

Not only that, but the toothpaste formed into a tiny version of Big Guy—complete with his big shoes and silly tie.

"Secret Agent Dingledorf!" Big Guy

shouted to me from my toothbrush.

"Not now," I said. "I've got problems of my own!"

"You mean Splat wanting to be a country-western singer?" he asked.

I frowned at the toothpaste. "How did you know?"

"The same way I know about the yodeling turtles," he said. "And the rapping snake. And all the animals that are singing in your city!"

"You know what's happening?" I asked.

The little toothpaste head nodded. "It's another plot by **B.A.D.D.**"

"You mean Bungling Agents Dedicated to Destruction?"

"Yes," he said. "They are trying to take over the world again."

"What is it this time?"

"They're feeding everyone's pets a secret

food. It makes the animals want to become singers and musicians."

I glanced over at Splat. For some reason he'd pulled a comb out of the bottom drawer. Now he was placing tissue paper against it.

I turned back to toothpaste, but the glob was melting back into a giant mound on my brush.

"How?" I asked.

"There's no time to explain. . . ." As the glob melted, so did the voice. "Come to Headquarters at once."

"But—" I started to argue.

BUUUZZZZ—BUZZZ—BUZZZ

I looked over at Splat. He'd made a strange musical instrument with the tissue paper and the comb. And by humming into it, he made an even stranger **B U Z Z Z**-ing noise.

"Hurry, Dingledorf. Hurr..."

That was all Big Guy said. Now he was just a blue blob of cavity-fighting fluoride.

I turned to Splat. His eyes were closed as he continued

BUUUZZZZ—BUZZZ—BUZZZ-ing.

I looked back at the giant glob of tooth-paste that used to be Big Guy.

I didn't want to do it. But I knew it was time to do the thing I didn't want to do but knew I had to do.

Translation: It was time to save the world . . . AGAIN.

CHAPTER 4

Sing a Song . . . Sort Of

Once again, it was time to save the world. (Don't you just hate it when that happens?)

Of course, some secret agents can't save the world without their parents' permission. Especially if those secret agents are in fourth grade.

But Dad was working late, and Mom had choir practice at church.

I could have called them. But that would mean using our phone. And my house has the same number of phone lines as bathrooms. And since I still have the same number of sisters, I knew calling anybody would be impossible.

So, I picked up Splat, who kept on

BURP-ing

while playing his comb and tissue paper instrument that kept on,

BUUUZZZZ—BUZZZ—BUZZZ-ing

and we headed for the church.

We arrived at the front steps and heard the music (if you could call it that). It was some of the worst

GROWLING,

YAPPING,

and

YOWLING

I had ever listened to. And for good reason.

Instead of people singing (which can be bad enough), it was their pets. That's right:

A German shepherd was dressed in chains and leather like a heavy-metal rock star. He ran around the stage **GROWLING**.

Two wiener dogs were dressed in way-too-skimpy tops like pop stars. They jumped up and down **YAPPING**.

And a bunch of cats were dressed in long black gowns like opera singers. They stood on their hind legs **YOWLING**.

I saw Mom sitting in the front pew. I ran to her shouting, "Mom, what's going on?"

"Isn't this terrible?" she shouted back.

"Yes!" I agreed.

"And that's just the first song." She pointed off to the side. "Look who's singing the next song."

I turned to see a pig dressed like a Broadway star. He was practicing going up and down the scales.

OiNK

OiNK　　OiNK

OiNK　　　　　　OiNK

OiNK　　　　　　　　OiNK

Beside him a goldfish swam in a bowl, dressed like Elvis.

BLUB

BLUB　　BLUB

BLUB　　　　　BLUB

BLUB　　　　　　　　BLUB

"What are we going to do?" Mom yelled. "Excuse me," Mrs. Spituna shouted. (She's the oldest member of our church.)

She hobbled past us, yelling, "My babies are singing next."

In her hands she held a giant ant farm—and the ants were also warming up.

CLICK

CLICK   *CLICK*

CLICK   *CLICK*

CLICK   *CLICK*

I turned back to Mom and shouted, "I have to go to Headquarters!"

"What?!" she yelled.

"I have to save the world again!"

"Okay!" She nodded in understanding. (Mom always understands about saving the world.) "Just be sure to wear clean underwear!" (Mom always worries about clean underwear.)

"Thanks!" I gave her a kiss. Then I

picked up Splat, who

BURP-ed.

From my arms, Splat grabbed his comb and tissue paper. We raced out of the church as he

BUUUZZZZ—BUZZZ—BUZZZ-ed

all the way.

We reached the sidewalk and came to a stop. Secret Headquarters was such a secret that even I didn't know where it was located.

They always picked me up.

But there was no one around.

No cars.

No planes.

No helicopters.

No nothing.

Nothing, except that tiny rain cloud about ten feet above our heads.

I looked up. How strange.

Stranger still was when it began to rain.

I turned to Splat. "What's going on?!"

"BURP. . . ." he burped.

Well, it was supposed to be a BURP.

But it's hard BURP-ing when you're busy melting.

BUSY MELTING?!

That's right. Before we knew it, the rain was dissolving us. Soon we had turned into a little puddle of Dingledorf and doggy goo.

A little puddle that quickly washed into the gutter and down into the storm drain.

```
A   B
U   U
G   U
  H   R
  H   R
  H   P
  H   P
  H   P...
```

SPLASH!

Of course, we did the usual thrashing around.

We were about to begin the usual drowning around when we got caught in a current.

We shot through the underground pipes. Faster and faster we went. And when we got tired of that we went faster some more.

Then, just when I was getting bored

and wished I'd brought a video game, we shot out of some kitchen faucet

S S
W P
I L
S I
H S
H

and landed in some kitchen sink.

splash!

(It would have been another **SPLASH!** but it was a tiny kitchen sink.)

CHAPTER 5

H.Q.

So there we were, just the two of us, splashing and swirling around in somebody's sink.

Suddenly, I heard Big Guy's voice. "Bring the Master Zapper."

A moment later some cool-looking machine was pointed at us.

Another moment later and that cool-looking machine was shooting out even cooler-looking

Vrrrrrrrrrrrrrrrrrrrrrr

beams of light.

Instantly, we became solid again. Everyone cheered.

We were pretty happy as we climbed out of the sink.

We would have been happier if the beam hadn't mixed us up!

Not a big problem, except . . . Splat now wore my shirt and tennis shoes. I now wore Splat's ring around the eye, and had his chubby belly.

"AHHH!" I shouted.

"BURP!" Splat burped.

"Sorry!" Big Guy said. "Let's try that again."

He turned the Master Zapper back on. The beam hit us.

Vrrrrrrrrrrrrrrrrrrrrr

And we were a lot better.

Well, almost.

Now there was the little problem of . . . Splat wearing my human ears and baseball hat. Me wearing Splat's droopy ears and stubby tail.

"AHHH!"

"BURP!"

"Sorry."

He tried one last time.

Vrrrrrrrrrrrrrrrrrrrr

Finally, we were back to normal. (Well, as normal as this secret agent and his trusty dog can be.)

"Hurry," Big Guy shouted. "There isn't much time!"

The three of us raced out of the kitchen and into the giant video room.

"You said **B.A.D.D.** is behind this?"

"Yes." Big Guy pressed a bunch of buttons. A video screen lowered.

Suddenly, we were looking at pets all across America. But these weren't your normal pets. Not anymore . . .

Bunnies were playing Mozart by hopping up and down on piano keyboards.

Hamsters were playing drums by banging on pots and pans with chopsticks.

And the ever popular parakeets? What else but chirping out silly lyrics from Saturday morning cartoon shows.

"How did this happen?" I asked.

Big Guy explained. "**B.A.D.D.** is giving the animals special food."

"But how?"

"Kids all over the country have quit being responsible. Instead of feeding their pets, they're letting other people do it."

"And those other people are . . ."

"The boys from **B.A.D.D.**"

"That's terrible," I said.

"No, that's **B.A.D.D.**," Big Guy said. "And you and Splat are the only ones who can save us."

"How?" I asked.

"With our new, special gizmos." He turned toward the door. "Come, let's head for the Gizmo Lab!"

The Gizmo Lab was as crazy as ever. The first scientist we saw was working on jet-propelled shoelaces. He lit the ends, stood back, and

whoosh-whoosh-whoosh- whoosh-whoosh-whoosh

until he flew out the window.

"Looks like it needs a little work," Big Guy said.

Another scientist was experimenting with Exploding Hiccup Powder. He added water, drank, and

Hic-cup
K-BOOM!!

"Looks like that needs a *lot* of work," I said.

We walked over to a table. It held all sorts of normal, everyday junk. (But I knew it was anything but normal and everyday.)

There was a new backpack, too. It had everything from school supplies to candy, food, and drinks.

There was also a new baseball cap.

"Are these all mine?" I asked as I tried on the cap.

Big Guy nodded. "Yes. They are the only way you can stop the—suddenly, he began to sing: *I came from Alabama, with my banjo on my knee, . . .*"

He frowned and cleared his throat. He tried again. "These are the only way you can stop—again he started singing: *I'm going to Louisiana, my true love for to see. . . .*"

"What's going on?" I asked.

Before Big Guy answered, a scientist joined him with a banjo.

The man played his banjo as Big Guy kept singing:

"*It rained all night the day I left, . . .*"
Soon other scientists joined in:
"*. . . the weather it was dry, . . .*"
"What's going on?" I repeated.
"They've gotten to us!" Big Guy gasped.
"What?" I shouted.
"They put the formula into *our* food. Hurry, grab your gizmos and get out before

it's too late!"

"But—"

"Hurry, before we begin the next verse!"

"Where do I begin?" I shouted. "Where do I look for—"

"The zoo!" he shouted. "Their headquarters is at the —*The sun so hot I froze to death,* —Hurry!— *Susanna, don't you cry.*"

I wasted little time and grabbed the stuff from the table.

I raced to Splat. He was busy giving autographs. I picked him up,

BURP

and we ran out of the building as Big Guy and the scientists started the chorus.

"Oh, Susanna, oh don't you cry for me. I've come from Alabama with my banjo on my knee."

The door slammed behind us.

Now all we had to do was get to the zoo! But how?

CHAPTER 6

A Hop, a Skip, and a Bounce

I reached into my new backpack. The first thing I pulled out was a handful of erasers.

"Oh, brother." I sighed.

I dropped them to the ground. But instead of falling and lying in the dirt, they

bounced.

And instead of bouncing once, they bounced again and again

higher ... and higher ... and higher.

I frowned. What good would they do?

I reached back into my pack and pulled out some bubblegum. The instructions on the wrapper read:

WARNING: Use only for sticking bouncing *erasers to your shoes.*

(I should have known.)

I popped the gum into my mouth and quickly

chomp, chomp, chomp-ed.

Then I caught as many of the bouncing erasers as I could.

I spit out the gum and stuck it to the bottom of my shoes (and to Splat's paws). Then I stuck the erasers to the gum.

"Well, here goes nothing," I said.

"Whimper," Splat whimpered. (At least he wasn't ᗷᑌᖇᑭ-ing or playing that stupid comb and paper anymore.)

We jumped into the air and landed on the ground. But instead of staying on the ground, we

bounced

higher . . . and higher . . . and higher.

Now all we had to do was bounce to the zoo. Right?

The only problem was, there were *three* problems:

1. We were at H.Q.

2. H.Q. was on a deserted island.

3. It's hard bouncing on water.

But I knew the Agency was good. I figured they had a solution. (At least I hoped they had a solution.)

We bounced to the end of the beach. Then we bounced as hard as we could and flew high into the air.

"AHHHHH!"
"WHIMPER, WHIMPER, WHIMPER!"

When we finally came down, it was just as I had hoped. We landed on the deck of an aircraft carrier!

"Good luck!" the sailors shouted.

"Bounce bounce," we bounced.

Again, we flew into the air. This time we came down on the back of a giant whale. It shouted in its best *Finding Nemo* voice:

"Mwwwyyyeeeeooooa!"

Again we sailed into the air. This time we flew so high that we had to dodge a flock of birds, not to mention a

ROARRR

747 or

ROARRR . . . ROARRR

two.

But as we came down I saw nothing to land on.

No boat, no whale, no nothing.

Quickly, I reached into my backpack and pulled out a piece of candy. But it was no ordinary candy. Once again I read the instructions:

Instant Island Maker: Just add water.

I threw the candy down as hard as I
could. It hit the water just a few seconds
before us. But those few seconds were all
it took.

A tiny island suddenly formed below
us . . . and just in time. We . . .

bounced

onto it, grabbed a coconut or two (Splat was hungry), and headed back up into the air.

This time we really flew high. So high that I could see the next bounce would bring us to dry land.

All we had to do was miss that asteroid

"LOOK OUT!"

"whimper, whimper!"

WhOOOOOOOOSH

and we would be safe.

CHAPTER 7

The Showdown

We missed the asteroid (**YEA!**).

We fell toward the ground at a gazillion miles an hour (**UH-OH!**).

Luckily, that's when my new baseball cap went into action. The front bill started spinning around, faster and faster,

whop-whop-whop-whop

until it turned into a helicopter!

(Actually, I guess it would be a . . . *hati*copter.)

Whatever it was, it stopped us from smashing into the ground.

I discovered that if I tilted my head one way or the other, I could steer. Soon, we were heading to the zoo.

But when we got there, the animals were already infected. We saw:

Alligators singing Cajun music;
Pandas singing Chinese songs; and
Lions singing—what else but hits
  from *The Lion King*.

Behind the cages I saw a bunch of dump trucks.

We flew over to investigate.

They were loading something into the trucks. I couldn't tell what until Splat started to

"whimper, whimper, whimper"

and then

drool, drool, drool.

I didn't understand the *whimper*-ing, but I understood the *drool*-ing. It meant we were near food!

We lowered closer.

Sure enough, one truck was loading dog food. Another was loading cat food. Another was loading bird food.

"Hey, you! Kid!"

I glanced down to see a mean-looking guy shouting up at us.

"What are you and that mutt doing?"

"Are you the **B.A.D.D.** guys?" I yelled.

All the truckdrivers looked up at us.

"What if we are?" Mean Guy shouted. "So what?"

"So, you can't make people feed your food to their pets!"

"We ain't makin' them do nothin'," he shouted. "People don't want to take responsibility, so we're doing it for them."

"No one likes responsibility," I shouted. "It's not fun!"

"Exactly!" he agreed. "But if you ain't willing to do it the *right* way, there's always somebody like me willing to do it the *wrong* way!"

I frowned. For a bad guy, he was making good sense.

He continued. "The world will have so many singing animals that they'll beg us to make them stop!"

"Will you?" I shouted.

"Of course." He looked at his truck-driving pals and smiled. "For a small fee."

"What type of fee?" I yelled.

"Oh, nothing much. Just taking over the world!" He let out a loud, mean-guy laugh:

"Moo-Hoo-Hoo-Haa-Haa-Haa . . ."

His bad-guy buddies joined in:

"Moo-Moo-Moo-Moo-Moo-Moo-Moo"
"Hoo-Hoo-Hoo-Hoo-Hoo-Hoo-Hoo"
"Haa-Haa-Haa-Haa-Haa-Haa-Haa"
    (He had a lot of buddies.)

Mean Guy shouted, "Now, go away before we hurt you!"
The "go away" part sounded good to Splat. Especially since his little body was still

"whimper, whimper, whimper"-ing.

It also sounded good to me. Especially since my little knees were

knock, knock, knock-ing.

But for some reason, leaving didn't seem right.

"What are you waiting for?" Mean Guy shouted.

"I have to stop you!"

"*YOU?! Stop US?!*"

There was another round of laughter. But instead of "*Moo*"-ing and "*Hoo*"-ing and "*Haa*"-ing, they laughed so hard they grabbed their sides. Then they threw themselves onto the ground and laughed some more.

"What's so funny?" I shouted.

Mean Guy yelled, "You're not responsible

enough to feed your dog. But you think you're responsible enough to save the world?!"

He had another good point . . . saving the world meant being responsible. But if I couldn't be responsible with little things (like feeding Splat), how could I be responsible for big things (like saving the world)?

"Now get outta here!" he shouted.

Did I want to leave?

You bet . . . big time.

But if I left, who would help the world? If I didn't do it the right way, somebody else (like Mean Guy) would do it the wrong way.

I hated to admit it, but it was time to be (here's that word again) . . .

RESPONSIBLE.

I pulled off my *hati*copter and threw it to the ground.

whop-whop-whop-whop

CRASH

Which means we quickly fell to the ground and also

CRASH-ed.

But that was the easy part.

Now came the hard part. Now we had to figure out what to do!

Big Guy saved us the trouble.

"AFTER THEM!" Mean Guy yelled.

We turned and saw the drivers racing toward us. Mean Guy grabbed a handful of food from a truck and shouted, "This is your last warning! Now's the time to turn and run away!"

"No!" I shouted back. "Now's the time to stay and be responsible!"

He threw back his head and let out another

"Moo-Hoo-Hoo-Haa-Haa-Haa . . ."

But two can play that game. I threw back my own head and also

"Moo-Hoo-Hoo-Haa-Haa-GULP!"

The *"Moo-Hoo-Haa"*-ing was me laughing.

The *GULP*-ing happened when Mean Guy threw the food into my mouth.

The food with the special formula.

The special formula that made me suddenly break out singing:

"WE *wish* you **a Merry** Christmas,
We *WISH* *you* A MERRY **Christmas."**

That's right. I had also fallen under the food's spell.

It made no difference that it was the middle of summer.

It made no difference that I was the worst singer in the world.

The point was . . . I no longer wanted to save the world. I no longer wanted to be responsible.

Now, all I wanted was to—

"WE *wish* you **a Merry** Christmas,
and a *Happy* **NEW** *Year!"*

CHAPTER 8

The Case Closes

The bad guys raced toward us.

I wanted to stop them, but I was right in the middle of singing:

"Oh, bring **us a** figgy *PUDDING,*
Oh, **BRING** US A figgy pudding, . . .**"**

I had no idea what a *"figgy pudding"* was, but it sounded like food. And food was something Splat understood. Not only did he understand it, he knew where to find it.

He crawled into my backpack and looked inside.

"Oh, bring us a figgy PUDDING,
AND bring it right here!"

The Mean Guy and his mean men had nearly reached us!

Lemon drop candy was the first thing Splat found. (Which meant it was the first thing he ate.)

But these were not ordinary lemon drops. They were so sour that he immediately

SPIT-SPIT-SPIT-SPIT

them out. But as they hit the ground, they immediately

K-Bang! K-Bamb! K-Pow!

exploded!

"Look out!" Mean Guy shouted.
They leaped to the side as Splat finished

SPIT-SPIT-SPIT-SPIT-ing

and

K-Bang! K-Bamb! K-Pow!-ing.

Meanwhile, I continued my concert:

"*We won't* **go** until *we* **GET** SOME,
We **WON'T** **GO** until **we get** SOME. . ."

The men leaped back to their feet and
started toward us.

Splat reached into my backpack and
pulled out some taco chips (with extra-hot
hot sauce).

He tore open the bag and began eating.

The chips looked good. But the hot sauce was a little hot. So hot that when Splat opened his mouth, he blew out flames twenty feet long!

K-*WHOOOOOOOOOOOOOOOOOOOOOOOOOOOOOOOSH*

"LOOK OUT!" Mean Guy shouted.

Suddenly, one of the trucks beside him caught fire and

K-BLEWIE!

exploded. And then two more.

K-BLEWIE! K-BLEWIE!

Now they were all catching fire and

K-BLEWIE! K-BLEWIE!
K-BLEWIE!

blowing up.

"Our food!" Mean Guy shouted. "You're destroying all our food!"

I nodded and answered:

"Good **TIDINGS** we bring,
TO YOU and your *kin*, . . ."

But Splat answered by digging back into my pack. His mouth was on fire from the sauce. There was only one way to put it out . . . with a can of juice.

He found the juice, opened it, and drank.

But this was no ordinary juice. This was green pepper juice! Which meant Splat suddenly began to . . .

BURPA-BURPA-BURPA.

"GRAB THEM!" Mean Guy shouted.

They surrounded us and closed in.

I still wanted to sing. But I also knew I had a responsibility to save my pudgy pal.

It was a tough decision, but I was finally learning my lesson.

I grabbed the can from Splat's hand and drank the rest of the juice. The **B.A.D.D.** boys were just a few feet away.

"Face the ground!" I shouted to Splat.

"BURP?" he burped.

"Yes!" I shouted. "Face the ground and start burping!"

He obeyed. We both looked down and started

BURPA-BURPA-BURP-ing.

We $Burp$-ed so hard and fast that we started rising into the air.

"More!" I shouted. "We need more $Burp$ power!"

He nodded. We bore down harder

BURPA-BURPA-BURPA

until we rose out of everyone's reach.

"Kid!" Mean Guy shouted. "You've ruined our plan to rule the world!"

I looked down at the trucks. He was right. They were all burning and exploding. All of the food had been destroyed.

Yes sir, it looked like we had once again saved the day (and the world while we were at it).

Well, actually, Splat had done the saving. I had just done the learning. But I had learned something very important. I

had learne [   ] importance of (here's
that word ag [   ] ‑ONSIBILITY.

With that [   ] of happy knowledge, we
turned and started

BURPA-BURPA-BURP-ing

for home.

The next morning everything was back
to normal. (Which at my house is like
saying everything was back to crazy.)

Once again my sisters were

Bang Bang Bang-ing

on the bathroom door and yelling at me to
get out.

Once again they practiced their morning shouting . . .

"Those are my shoes!"

"That's my scarf!"

"That's my coat!"

And once again they **ZOOMED**, *SWISHED*, and **WHOOSHED** past Mom at the breakfast table.

Of course, Dad and I didn't want to hurt Mom's feelings. So we were happy to eat all the leftovers. (I was even happier that she didn't serve green pepper juice.)

Then I grabbed my books, kissed her, and raced for the door.

"Don't forget to feed Splat!" she called.

This time I didn't complain. This time I stopped and filled Splat's dish with food and gave him fresh water.

I watched as he gobbled it up in his usual 2½ seconds.

"Attaboy," I said. I patted him on the head and stopped to think.

It's true. Responsibility isn't always easy. Sometimes it's downright hard.

beep-beep-beep-beep

But it's something we all have to learn. Something we all have to practice.

I turned to Splat. "Isn't that right, boy?"

"BURP," he burped.

beep-beep-beep-beep

And right now it sounded like I'd get to practice it again by

beep-beep-beep-beep

answering my underwear.

ALSO FROM BILL MYERS . . .

The Incredible Worlds of Wally McDoogle

A series about Bernie Dingledorf's older cousin Wally
McDoogle, also known as boy blunder, master of mayhem,
and Wally-the-Walking-Disaster-Area. Follow Wally as he
stumbles through one wacky adventure after another.

MY LIFE AS A SMASHED BURRITO WITH EXTRA HOT SAUCE
An Excerpt

Don't get me wrong, Camp Wahkah Wahkah
wasn't the worst experience I've ever had. I
mean, when you're the shortest kid in sixth
grade, forced to wear Woody Allen glasses all
your life, and basically serve as the all-school
punching bag, you've got lots of bad experiences
to choose from. But Camp Whacko (that's what
we called it for short) definitely rated right up
there in the top ten.

I knew I was in trouble the moment I stepped
onto the camp bus. Of course it was full of the
usual screaming crazies. No surprise there. I
mean, you take the politest kid in the world and
put him on a camp bus, and he goes bonkers.
Count on it. It's like a law or something. What
caught me off guard was the flying peanut butter and jelly sandwich . . . open faced, of course.
I tried to duck, but I was too late.

K-THWACK! right in the old kisser. Fortunately, the jelly was grape, my favorite. And by the gentle aroma of freshly baked peanuts, I knew the peanut butter had to be Skippy. Another lucky break. What was not lucky was that it completely covered my glasses. I couldn't see a thing.

Before I knew it, the bus ground into gear and lurched forward. Everyone cheered. Well, almost everyone. I was busy stumbling down the aisle at record speed. Of course, there were the usual "Smooth move, Dork Breath" and "Way to go, McDoogle" as I tumbled past. (What a comfort to hear familiar voices in time of trouble.)

Then I got lucky. Through the peanut butter I caught a glimpse of an empty seat toward the back. It took a little doing and bouncing off a couple campers—"Oh, ick!" "Get away, Geek!" (more of my old school chums)—but I finally managed to crash into the empty seat.

Whew. Safe at last. Well, not exactly . . .

As I peeled the bread off my face and removed my glasses, I noticed that the whole bus had grown very quiet. I quickly scraped the peanut butter and jelly gunk off of my glasses and into my hands. Then I pushed my glasses back on.

I wished I hadn't.

The first thing I noticed was that all eyes were on me.

The second thing I noticed was a thick crackly

voice. A voice that sounded like it ate gravel for lunch and then washed it down with a box of thumbtacks.

But that was nothing compared to the third thing I noticed—the fierce-sounding, gravelly voice was directed at *ME*.

"You're sitting in my seat."

I turned to see who was talking.

Another mistake. Sometimes if you're going to die, it's best not to know the details. But by recognizing the kid's face and noticing the size of his biceps, I not only knew the "who," I knew the "how."

It was Gary the Gorilla. He hated that name. In fact, he did bodily harm to anyone he heard using it. But it was all anyone knew him by. We'd never officially met, but I recognized his picture from the papers. Or maybe it was the post office. Or maybe both. It didn't matter where. The point is, once you saw it you never forgot it. And you'd always go out of your way to avoid it.

That's okay, I thought. Don't panic. Turn on some of that world-famous McDoogle charm. Be his friend. Yeah, that's it. The poor guy's probably just misunderstood. Maybe if somebody reached out to him and tried—

"Hi there," I said, reaching to shake his hand. "My name is Wally McDoogle. I'm, uh . . ."

I don't know whether I stopped because of the look on his face or the gasps from the crowd. But when I glanced down at our handshake, I saw the problem. I had just transferred all of the peanut butter and jelly gunk from my hand into his.

"Oh, sorry, Mr. Gorilla, . . . er, that is, I mean . . ."

With one swift move he had me by the collar. Next, I was high above his head and pressed tightly to the ceiling of the bus.

Suddenly, my whole life passed before my eyes. Well, it wasn't my whole life. Mostly just the part of how I got into this predicament. It all started with Dad less than eight weeks ago . . .

"Don't worry," he shouted, leaning over the lawn mower as I fought to empty the grass catcher. "Church camp will be great for you."

"But Dad—"

"Especially that two-day canoe trip—get you out in the wild away from the luxuries of the big city—"

"But Dad—"

"New challenges, new adventures—"

"Dad."

"And the most important thing of all . . ."

Uh-oh, I thought, *here it comes.*

"It will make you a real man."

"A real man." That seemed to be Dad's whole purpose in my life lately. Maybe it had to do

with him being All-State something or other back in his high school football days. Or maybe it was because Burt and Brock, my older twin brothers, win every sports trophy they can get their sweaty paws on. Or maybe it was because I made the mistake of telling everybody at dinner one night that I wanted to be a writer.

"A writer?" Dad winced.

"Yeah, but not just a writer—a screenwriter. You know, like movies and stuff."

"Yeah, but . . . *a writer?*" The word stuck in his throat like Aunt Martha's overcooked chicken.

"Sure, lots of people do that."

"But . . . a writer?"

Less than four weeks later, the brochure from Camp Whacko mysteriously showed up on my dresser. It wasn't long before the camp found its way into our daily conversations. It made no difference how I argued. Somehow, someway, just four weeks later, I found myself loading my bags into the car and heading for the church bus.

"You sure you need that computer thing?" Dad asked as he suspiciously eyed the laptop computer I was carrying to the car.

"Sure Dad." I tried to sound matter of fact. "It will, uh, um, it will help me take notes on all the outdoorsy stuff I learn."

"Hmmm . . ." was all he said.

I pulled the computer closer to my side. This could get messy.

He stood beside the car and slowly crossed his arms.

"Please, God," I silently prayed, *"not Ol' Betsy, too."* ("Betsy," that's what I call my computer.)

Finally, Mom spoke up. "I think he should take it, Herb. It's one thing to ship the boy off to camp against his will, but to take away his computer?"

"I didn't say we should," Dad hedged. "It's just with all the new experiences he'll be having, I wonder if it's really necessary to—"

"I *really* think he should take it, Herb."

Now, everyone in our family knows what it means when Mom says *"really"* like that. It means her mind is made up. Oh sure, Dad could still have his way—after all, he is the man of the house. But if he did, it meant he'd have to pay for it in the days to come. Little things like cold dinners, burnt toast, or finding starch in his underwear. You know, details like that.

"It was just a suggestion," he offered as he threw the rest of my bags into the trunk.

"Thanks, Mom." I grinned and climbed into the car.

"No sweat, Kiddo," she said, sticking her head through the open window and giving me a good-bye kiss. "But you owe me."

"Put it on my bill."

Dad started the car, but before we pulled away, Mom went down her list of usual "Mom" things. You know, stuff like, "I expect you to wear your pajamas. Tops *and* bottoms."

"Yes, Mom."

"And don't forget to change your underwear."

"Yes, Mom."

"And don't forget to floss. Remember, healthy gums are happy gums."

"Son . . ." Now it was Dad's turn. But instead of a long lecture he reached over, put his powerful hand on my shoulder, and looked me straight in the eyes. I knew it was going to be something profound, something deeply moving, something I'd remember the rest of my life.

"Son," he repeated to build the suspense. Then after a deep breath he continued. "Think . . . *manly* thoughts."

I did my best to smile. He gave me a reassuring nod, put the car in gear, and off we headed for the bus.

That was just half an hour ago. And now, thirty short minutes later, I was pinned to the roof of the bus by Gary the Gorilla.

So this is what it feels like to die? I thought. Not so bad. Course, it would be better if he'd let go of my collar so I could breathe. Still, on the McDoogle pain scale of 1 to 10 this is only a—

Suddenly, an idea came to mind. I reached down to his meaty hand (the one wrapped around my throat) and scraped the rest of the peanut butter and jelly from it. Next I began to eat the stuff. The idea was to get him to laugh, to show him that I was just a stupid geek and that this was all just a stupid geek accident.

Unfortunately, he didn't laugh. But the rest of the bus did. And as they chuckled, Gary, being the insecure kind of bully he was, naturally thought they were laughing at him.

His grip around my neck tightened.

Now, I've got to admit, I don't exactly remember praying. Sometimes when you're busy dying you forget little details like that. But suddenly, out of the blue, I heard this voice:

"Put him down, Gary."

At first I thought it was God, or at least one of those archangel guys we hear about in Sunday school. After all, this was a church bus going to a church camp. But when I turned I saw it was only a counselor. Still, beggars can't be choosers. I'd take what I could get.

Gary gave the man a glare but the counselor stayed cool and calm.

"Put him down," the man repeated.

I gave my glasses a nervous little push back onto my nose. Unfortunately, it was with the hand still dripping in peanut butter and jelly. I noticed an exceptionally large glob of the goo starting to fall. I tried to catch it but I was too late.

K-SPLAT!

From high above it nailed Gorilla Boy right in the ol' face.

The bus broke into even louder laughter.

Gary never had people laugh at him—at least not to his face—at least no one who lived to tell about it. And to have it happen twice in a row was unthinkable. But instead of enjoying the experience as something to treasure and remember, Gary turned beet red. The muscles in his neck began to tighten and quiver.

Find out what happens next!

Read

MY LIFE AS A SMASHED BURRITO WITH EXTRA HOT SAUCE

You'll want to read them all.

The Incredible Worlds of Wally McDoogle

#15—*My Life As a Human Hairball*
(ISBN 0-8499-4024-9)

#16—*My Life As a Walrus Whoopee Cushion*
(ISBN 0-8499-4025-7)

#17—*My Life As a Computer Cockroach*
(formerly My Life As a Mixed-Up Millennium Bug)
(ISBN 0-8499-4026-5)

#18—*My Life As a Beat-Up Basketball Backboard*
(ISBN 0-8499-4027-3)

#19—*My Life As a Cowboy Cowpie*
(ISBN 0-8499-5990-X)

#20—*My Life As Invisible Intestines*
(ISBN 0-8499-5991-8)

#21—*My Life As a Skysurfing Skateboarder*
(ISBN 0-8499-5992-6)

#22—*My Life As a Tarantula Toe Tickler*
(ISBN 0-8499-5993-4)

#23—*My Life As a Prickly Porcupine from Pluto*
(ISBN 0-8499-5994-2)

#24—*My Life As a Splatted-Flat Quarterback*
(ISBN 0-8499-5995-0)

Now on CD

the incredible worlds of Wally McDoogle
audio

Vol. 1: *My Life As a Smashed Burrito and Other Misadventures*
(includes *Alien Monster Bait*)
(ISBN 0-8499-3402-8)

Vol. 2: *My Life As a Broken Bungee Cord and Other Misadventures*
(includes *Crocodile Junk Food*)
(ISBN 0-8499-3402-8)

SECRET AGENT DINGLEDORF

... and his trusty dog, SPLAT 🐾

BY BILL MYERS

OTHER BOOKS IN THIS SERIES

1—The Case of the Giggling Geeks

The world's smartest people can't stop laughing. Is this the work of the crazy criminal Dr. Chuckles? Only Secret Agent Dingledorf (the country's greatest agent, even if he is only ten years old) can find out . . . while discovering the importance of respecting and loving others. (ISBN: 1-4003-0094-0)

2—The Case of the Chewable Worms

The earth is being invaded by worms! And, worst of all, people find them . . . tasty! But is it really the work of B.A.D.D. (Bungling Agents Dedicated to Destruction)? Will Dingledorf and Splat realize the importance of doing good and helping others in time to solve the case? (ISBN: 1-4003-0095-9)

3—The Case of the Flying Toenails

It started out with one lie. Now, everybody is coming down with the dreaded jet-powered toenails disease! Will Dingledorf and Splat discover how important it is to be honest and tell the truth in time to stop the dreaded disease? (ISBN: 1-4003-0096-7)

4—The Case of the Drooling Dinosaurs

The museum's dinosaurs have come alive, and they're on the move, slobbering everywhere. Only Dingledorf and Splat can find the answer and save the day . . . but first they must learn the importance of obeying the rules. (ISBN: 1-4003-0177-7)

5—The Case of the Hiccupping Ears

People all over the world are forgetting to eat, see, talk, hear, smell, and even walk! Dingledorf and Splat learn how wonderfully God has made the human body as they work to solve the mysterious case. (ISBN: 1-4003-0178-5)